A BOOK

CRABTREE

BY JON &
TUCKER
NICHOLS

FOR
RUBY
AND
ADA

LOST TEETH

CALL ALFRED

One bright fall day, Alfred Crabtree woke up
to discover he couldn't find his false teeth.

He tried posting a LOST TEETH sign at the local
post office, but he was afraid nobody would see it.

So Alfred started searching his belongings himself.

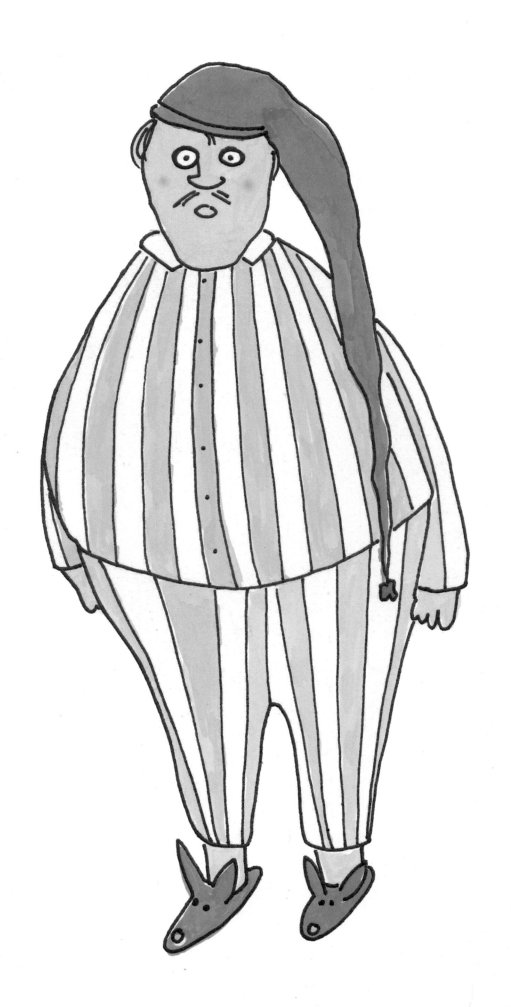

artichoke

Wiffle ball

HUGE BUBBLE

gum

RUPERT'S

chickadee

peas

bugle

grasshopper

tape, Scotch

drum stick (left)

weed

spout

handle

fish can

Sorry

fire extinguisher

from San Antonio

blueberry muffin

Master Lock

Timothy's chair

gas can

for cleaning the gutters

croissant

Lego

unripe

stinkin' badge

egg shell

earplug (right)

Alfred had a lot of belongings.

SHOE POLISH
BROWN BROWN BROWN
for shiny shoes

shoe for
Irma's horse

cheese slicer

hose nozzle

air pump

spray can

WD40

spyglass

earthworm

So he called his sister Myrna.
She said, "Alfred, you need to get organized.
Put everything you have into categories.
Anything left over will be
your missing teeth."

drum stick (right)

mustache comb

DO RENTALS

coat hanger

beans

LIMA BEANS

HOT SAUCE

squeeze bottle

keychain

ENGLISH MUFFINS

talkie

seahorse

safety pin

CHAP STICK

lip stuff

SHAM POO

squeeze bottle

blue boot

Friday

Saturday

also Saturday

ear

HATS & HELMETS

witch

woot

wizard

watch out

for my moped

for welding

Tex

So Alfred put everything into categories. He started with his hats and helmets. If something was a hat or a helmet, he put it with all of the other hats and helmets.

FLAVOR PACKET

for mac & cheese

bottle caps

SODA

POP

pull tab

B: THREE DOG NIGHT

tape, cassette

DUCKS

pennant

Kiss

snow globe

chalk for pool

plunger

walkie

Viewmaster disc

FLYING MONKEYS

He spread his things out to examine them more closely. But it was confusing, looking at all of his things like this. And messy. He needed advice.

lobster claw

nine volts

for finding spiders

canoe engine

tarantula

spare key

earplug (left)

black   razz

full

hourglass

HALF AND HALF

paint can

MOST IMPROVED

PADDLE TENNIS

goblet

GOLDEN GATE PAINT

Velma's trophy

fly spatula

WAWA

Q-tip

REAL DUCKS

Next, he put his ducks and decoys together with his other ducks and decoys. No teeth yet, but at least his ducks and decoys were organized!

DECOYS

mobile decoy unit

bills

threaded neck

two-legged

tan head

purple head

streamlined

masked

spare eyeballs

floater

most of my aunts

silly hat day

Grandma (close up)

Jabez Hatch

Myrna

Irma

from the old country

doorbell

porthole

Then he put all of his family portraits together.

PORTRAITS

Lincoln at picnic with books

at Sutro Baths

Velma

photobooth

Nut

a proud moment

Burp, Slurp, and Sigmund

graduation

with Boom

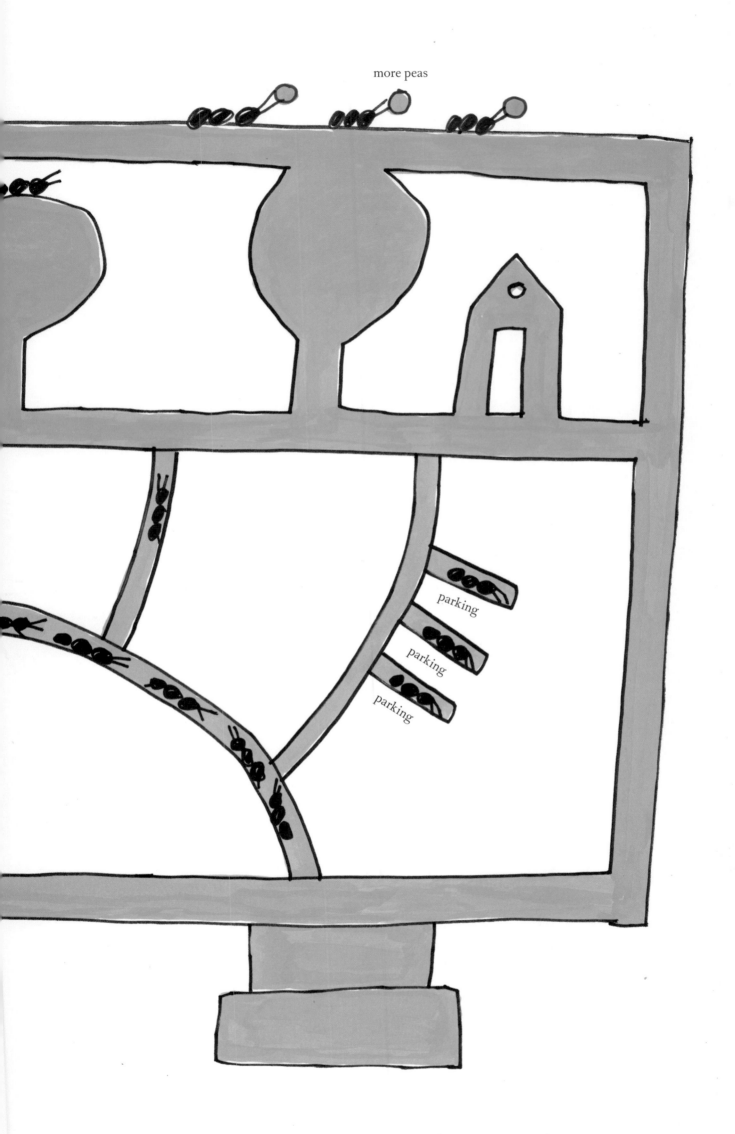

He put his ants together in an ant farm.

old tools

INSTRUCTION
BOOKLET

to what?

Velma's house key

Smitty's stick

from Irma's cake

paintbrush

hot dog bun

tangle

nails

squeeze bottle

He put his tools and
utensils together.

He put all of his favorite food together.
This was a hard step, because it made him hungry.

Yentl's lentils

brussels sprouts with mussels, trouts

Spam and a yam

mustard on custard

falafel with tall waffle

poodle and noodle

dip on a chip

can of peas with a slice of cheese

ham with mint jam

It is no fun to be hungry
when you are looking for
your false teeth.

itchy

scratchy

rolled sock balls

stinky

olive

tube, left

missing thumb

handball, left

winter, left

SOCKS & MITTENS

He put his socks and mittens together. Alfred was really getting the hang of this! But now everything was so spread out, he could barely move.

winter, right

grey

glewed by Beefeater

darned

too small

good for dishes

stretchy

bad for snowballs

striped

tube, also left

knee

He needed more advice! So he called his sister Irma. She said, "Alfred, put your things in boxes. That way, you'll have room to move."

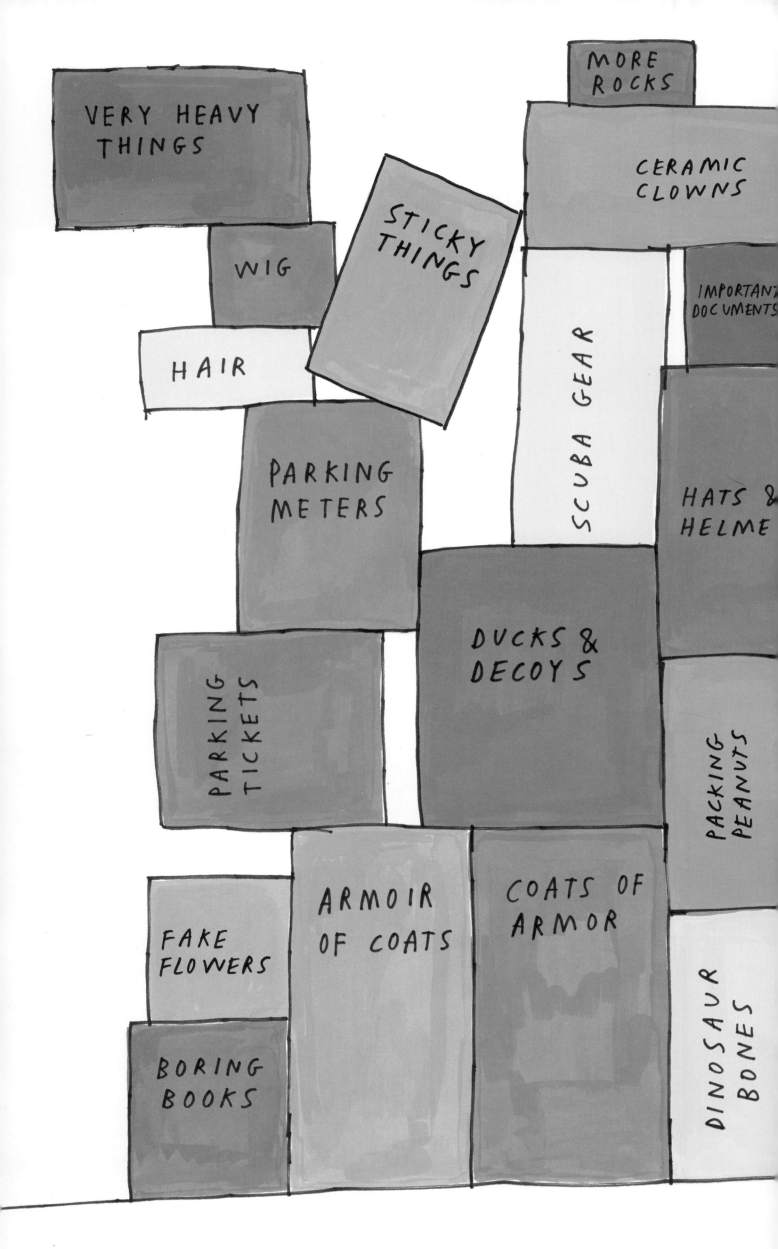

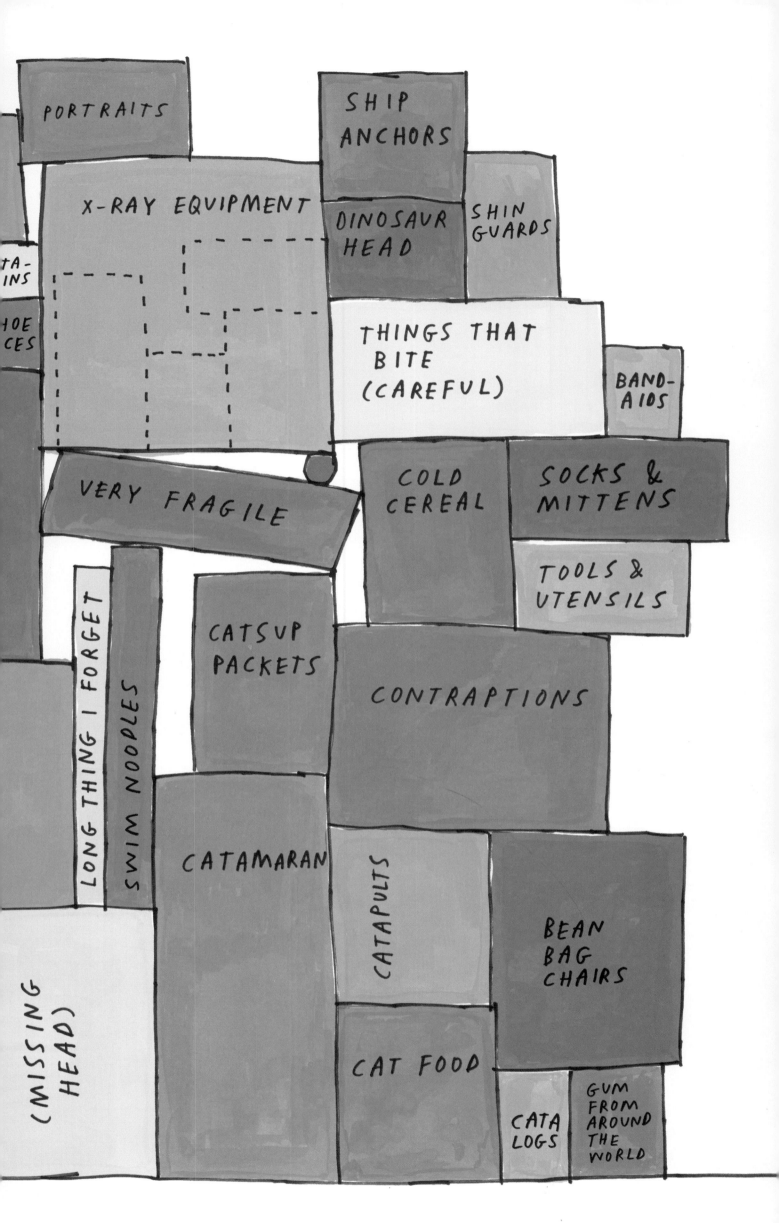

So Alfred Crabtree began putting everything he had in boxes.
Stacking the boxes gave him room to keep searching.

bus

my favorite pants

WHITENING PASTE

turns yellow things white

MAIL

Irma's PO box

Buddy's glasses

Myrna's house?

feather

fix-it shop

GARAGE

butterfly

fake flower

He put all of his yellow things in a box.

regular pencil

giant pencil

crown

rock

potato

tennis ball

gecko

stack of lemons

SPICY DIJON

squeeze bottle

chickpeas

Fred

UN PESO

coin

Fred

mustachio

YELLOW

dressy

winter casual

Gideon

generally
misbehaves

Mouse

is sweet

Howard

Beefeater

wants people food

Sebastian

Mrs. Wilmerding

shakes hands

Chestnut

Muffet

Emma

always
looks guilty

Tito

plays
with birds

Dora has an

dirty
tennis balls

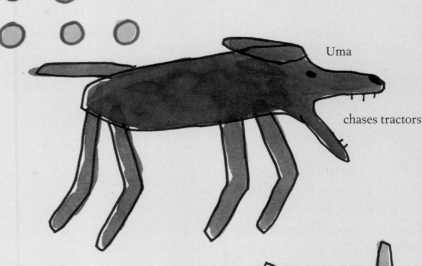

SMALL YAPPING DOGS

Uma

chases tractors

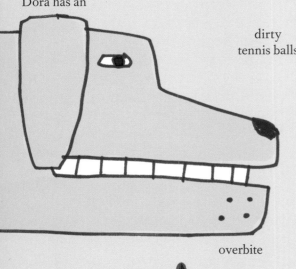

overbite

Smitty

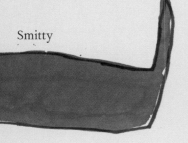

naps a lot

Powder the cat

shouldn't be in here

Ananda

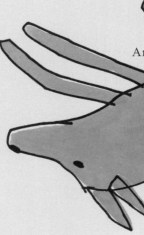

howls at airplanes

Daffy

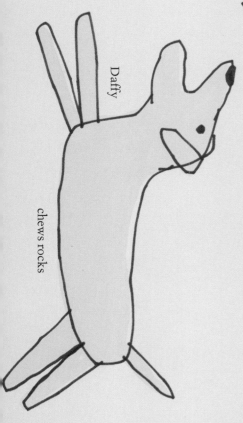

chews rocks

Baeos

tries harder

He put his small
yapping dogs
in a box.

that dog

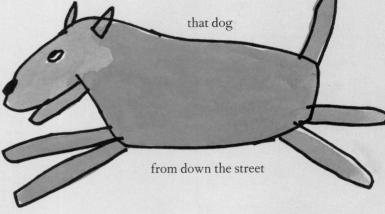

from down the street

sardines

suitcase

sausage

slug

seal stamp

54

sculpture

salt

SUDSY

soap

snowballs

smudge

S

ski boot

seventh scallop

snake

spoon

sneaker

shoe

staples

skate

Speedo

sweat socks

He put everything that started with S in a box.

coat hanger

TAKE A VACATION

coat hanger

None of this was easy.
So Alfred took a little break to watch some TV.

six scallops

mac
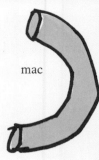

SHELLS

pistachios

Sally's turtle
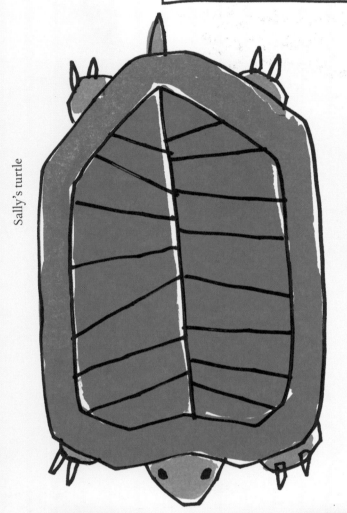

horseshoe
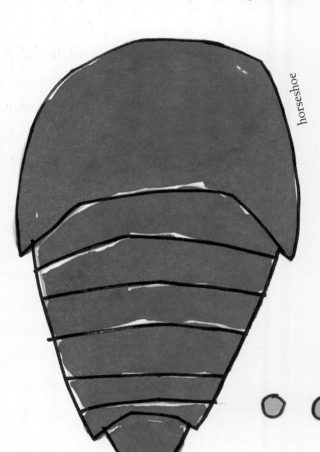

REAL ITALIAN PASTA

conchiglioni

hermit

nut
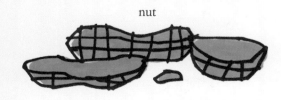

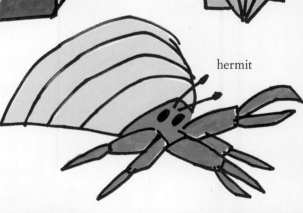

crab

egg

conch

tiny snail jar

super slow

armadillo

Then he put all of his shells in a box.

He packed all of his broken things in a box.

it keeps growing

(top view)

smells like honeysuckle

too small

from Barcelona

rattles when you shake it

gift from Myrna

still works like new

Alfred didn't even know what
the things in the next box were.
He was feeling pretty worn down.
But he still had to find his teeth.

from the barn

from the garage

from the attic

I DON'T KNOW WHAT THESE THINGS ARE

free when I opened bank account

very heavy

these

fell out of here

from under bed

He needed more advice! So he called his sister Velma. She said, "Um, Alfred, did you try looking for your teeth in your TEETH CLOSET?"

narwhal

Bluetooth headset

lucky toothbrush

unlucky toothpaste

very old vampire tooth

Dracula

leopard teeth

happy tooth pin

cog teeth

bird beak

Tootsie Pop

hey, my teeth

fake smile

snack

Chopper

mastodon (left)

gecko tooth

decoy bills

walrus tusks

saw teeth

alligator teeth

scrimshaw

lost

toothfish

jaguar tooth

wind-up chompers

The teeth closet! Of course! Alfred looked in the closet,
found his teeth, and popped them in his mouth.
He also found a snack there, which he gobbled up.

Rocko's tooth

real smile

Chiclets

lion tooth

press-on nail

candy corn

Bugs

possibly rocks

Jaws

Jaws 2

Jaws 3

Daffy's teeth

spearmint Tic Tacs

TEETH

earplug

spare floss

cheetah teeth

cougar tooth

Cro-Magnon

retainer

poker

prodder

hook

rear view

extractor

mini marshmallows

caveman teeth

lost in an apple

fossilized teeth

tooth fairy

money

mastodon (right)

wisdom tooth

roller derby mouthguard

bobcat tooth

braces

lost in a sledding accident

Tito's tooth

CHAMPION DENTISTRY OPEN

Specimen A

Specimen B

Specimen Q

salt water taffy

dentist sign

mouthwash

under pillow

teeth dish

TOOTH POWDER

powder can

unicorn

ship

"Phew!" Alfred said. "I need a break!"

Just then, a big false-teeth grin spread across his face.
He had an idea! He'd take a vacation cruise!

So Alfred Crabtree loaded all of his
boxes onto a cargo ship, climbed aboard,
and went away for the weekend.

He brought only the most important things.